6/13

REBOUND TIME

BY **JAKE MADDOX**

text by Emma Carlson Berne
illustrated by Katie Wood

STONE ARCH BOOKS
a capstone imprint

Jake Maddox books are published by Stone Arch Books
A Capstone Imprint
1710 Roe Crest Drive
North Mankato, Minnesota 56003
www.capstonepub.com

Library of Congress Cataloging-in-Publication Data is available on
the Library of Congress website.

Summary: Can Sarit learn to love playing basketball without her dad
on the sidelines?

ISBN 978-1-4342-4013-2 (library binding)
ISBN 978-1-4342-4202-0 (pbk.)

Designer: Kristi Carlson
Production Specialist: Laura Manthe

Printed in China by Nordica.
1012/CA21201278
092012   006935NORDS13

TABLE OF CONTENTS

Chapter One

A HARD ADJUSTMENT

Sitting on a bench in the Greenville Middle School locker room, Sarit leaned down and laced up her white basketball shoes. The locker room was full of girls getting ready for the first basketball practice of the new season. They were all laughing and chattering excitedly.

But Sarit was silent. She didn't want to go out onto the court. Ever since her dad had moved across the country, she didn't want to play at all.

Her twin sister, Allie, looked over at her. "Hey, it's okay," Allie said. "I know it'll be hard to practice without Dad, but Coach Ritz seems really nice."

Sarit didn't reply. She didn't understand why her sister wasn't more upset. Their father had been the coach for their basketball team, the Cowboys, since they'd started playing in fourth grade.

But then last year their parents had divorced, and their dad had moved to the other side of the country for a new job.

Sarit had never played basketball without her father on the court. She wasn't even sure she knew how to play without him there. Basketball practice was the time they'd always spent together. Now he was gone. Basketball was still there, but it no longer seemed like any fun.

"Come on, guys, Coach wants to start!" one of the players called. The other girls hurried out of the locker room. Sarit didn't move.

"Aren't you coming out?" Allie asked, looking worried.

Sarit nodded. "Just give me a minute, okay?" she said quietly. "I'll be right there. Promise."

"Okay," Allie said slowly. "I'll be on the court." With one final, worried look at her sister, Allie followed the rest of the team out of the locker room.

Sarit stayed on the bench in the empty locker room after her sister left. Through the door, she could hear the new coach's voice calling out instructions as the team ran drills. He sounded nice enough.

Sarit sighed and stood up. *Maybe Allie's right,* she thought. *Maybe I just need to give the new coach a chance.*

The rest of the team was busy running a passing drill when Sarit walked into the gym. The girls were all breathing hard as they dribbled back and forth across the court.

At one end of the court, Coach Ritz stood, holding his clipboard and a whistle. "Let's see some hustle out there, girls!" he yelled to the team. "Keep those balls under control!"

Dad never yelled at us, Sarit thought. But deep down she knew that wasn't really true. Coach Ritz was just doing his job.

But it should still be Dad standing there, like always, she thought miserably.

Coach Ritz spotted her. "Hey, Sarit," he called. "Find a place in line." His voice was gentle. He knew about the situation with her dad.

Sarit nodded and slipped in line behind her sister. Allie smiled and handed her a basketball.

Fwweet! The coach blew his whistle loudly.

At the sound, the girls in the front of the line ran forward, dribbling the balls in front of them as they went. When they reached the end of the court, they spun and dribbled back.

Sarit stared down at the ball in her hands. She'd always loved the feel of holding a basketball. It felt right in her hands, like an old, familiar friend.

But today, the ball felt awkward, like it was too big somehow. She didn't know what to do with it. Her hands were sweating, and her grip on the ball was slippery.

Sarit thought about what her dad had told her when they'd practiced dribbling on the driveway last year.

"The trick is to keep your eyes straight ahead and not think too much about your hands," he'd told her. "Let your hands do the work, not your head."

Fweet! The next line of players ran forward toward the end of the court. Allie ran ahead of the others, dribbling easily. She was always the fastest runner. Anna, the center, was close behind. Suddenly, Anna lost control of the ball. She had to break from the line to retrieve it.

Allie reached the end of the court first. Sarit watched her effortlessly reverse direction, backing up a few feet, while still keeping the basketball close to her and in play.

"Good work, Allie!" Coach Ritz yelled. "Everyone, keep the ball close! That's the trick. As you back up, bring the ball with you."

Sarit took a deep breath. Her line was next. *Come on,* she told herself. *Allie's playing fine. You can too.* She gritted her teeth as the coach's whistle blew one more time.

Chapter Two

NOTHING FEELS THE SAME

Sarit forced herself to run forward, dribbling the ball in front of her. She focused on the other end of the gym. All she had to do was get through the practice.

It's only an hour, she thought. *I can do this.* But her feet felt clumsy and slow, like her sneakers were filled with cement. She almost lost control of the ball but managed to capture it before it rolled away. She made it to the end. Now for the back-up.

Let your hands do the work, she thought. *Just like Dad always said.*

With her feet scissoring along the floor, Sarit reversed direction, bringing the ball with her. She spun on her foot, still dribbling, and started back toward the starting line.

"Good work, Sarit!" she heard Allie holler.

Sarit ran down the court. Her palms were slick with sweat. Even this simple drill felt harder than it usually did. She could see the coach standing under the hoop at the other end, his whistle at his lips.

A trickle of sweat ran into her eyes, blurring her vision. For a moment, she thought she saw a tall man standing near the basket.

Dad! Sarit thought. But she knew he wasn't really there. Sarit was so focused on the other end of the court that she tripped, and the ball flew out of her hands. It bounced into a far corner of the gym.

Sarit stopped. The figure of her dad had disappeared. It was only Coach Ritz standing there. Sarit could feel everyone staring at her as she stood in the middle of the gym floor.

"Hey, Sarit, take five minutes, okay?" Coach Ritz called out.

She could tell he was trying to be nice, but it just made Sarit feel worse. Tears pricked her eyes. She knew she was going to cry.

I have to get out of here, Sarit thought frantically. *I can't do this.*

She took off running toward the gym doors. She hit the push bar hard. The doors flew open, banging against the brick wall. She ran down the hallway and out of the building.

The sun glared down on the sidewalk outside. Sarit ran onto the athletic field and stopped near the bleachers. She sat down, rested her forehead against her knees, and cried.

After a minute, Sarit felt a hand settle gently on her back. She raised her head. Allie was standing behind her, looking concerned.

"Hey," Allie said softly. She sat down next to Sarit and slipped an arm around her shoulders. "Coach wanted me to see how you were doing."

Sarit sniffled and swiped at her wet cheeks with the back of her hand. "Terrible," she said. "I don't want to go back in there."

Allie took Sarit's hand. "Don't worry about fumbling the ball," she said. "It was just a drill. Who cares? You'll do better next time."

Sarit shook her head. "It's not that," she said. "I don't care about the drill. It's Dad. Nothing feels the same without him there."

Her throat ached, and for a second, Sarit thought she would start crying again. "I don't even want to play," she whispered.

"You'll feel better in a minute," Allie encouraged her. She picked up her water bottle and held it out to Sarit. "Maybe you should have some water," she said.

Sarit pushed the bottle away. "You don't understand," she replied. Her voice was getting louder. "I don't want to play without Dad. Ever!" She was practically shouting. "You're just playing like Dad never left. You don't even care that he's not here!"

Allie started at her, wide-eyed. She opened her mouth to reply, but Sarit turned away. She didn't want to hear what Allie had to say.

Sarit whirled around and ran across the grass. She didn't even know what she was running away from. Coach Ritz? The basketball court? Her sister? All Sarit knew was that she wanted to be far, far away.

Chapter Three

THE LIES KEEP COMING

Sarit ran almost the whole way home. When she got to the corner of her street, she paused. She could see her mom out in front of their house, pruning the bushes. Sarit ducked behind a mailbox and wiped her face off with her T-shirt. She didn't want her mom to see how upset she was.

"Hi, Mom," Sarit said, casually walking up the driveway. *Please don't let her look up,* she thought.

She was almost to the front door when her mother stopped her. "Aren't you supposed to be at basketball practice today?" Mom asked. "Why are you home from practice so early?"

Sarit stopped. She turned around slowly. Her mother stood behind her, waiting. Sarit didn't want to talk, but she knew her mom wouldn't just let it go.

"Um, the new coach let us out early," Sarit finally said. Her cheeks felt hot. She normally didn't lie.

Mom frowned. "Where is your sister?" she asked.

"Oh, she stayed to scrimmage with some of the other girls," Sarit said. She felt like her mom could see right through her. But her mother was already turning away.

"All right," Mom said. "Dinner is at six o'clock."

"Okay," Sarit replied. "I'll be in my room." She went inside and closed the door to her room. Then she sank down on her bed with a sigh.

She thought about how much fun she'd had playing basketball with her dad and Allie last summer. They'd played two-on-one on the driveway almost every weekend. Mom had always had to remind them to come in when it got dark.

One Saturday in particular, she and Allie had teamed up to play against Dad. Dad had been guarding the basket. Sarit darted left and right, trying to throw him off. Then she'd gone in for a lay-up. She ran for the basket and jumped. Dad had been in front of her, but she'd spun around to avoid him.

Sarit remembered slamming the ball through the basket. It had been the best feeling in the whole world.

Dad had caught the ball on the rebound. "I never should have taught you that spin," he'd said, laughing. "It's coming back to haunt me."

Allie had laughed too. Then Dad threw her the ball, and she'd thrown it back to Sarit. The basketball game had turned into keep-away, with Dad in the middle. All of them had laughed so hard they could hardly stand up.

The phone on her bedside table rang, interrupting Sarit's daydream. She picked up the phone and saw her dad's number on the display. She answered right away.

"Hi, sweetie," her father said.

Sarit almost started crying again at the sound of her father's voice. But she managed to swallow the tears. "Hi, Dad," she replied. Her voice sounded almost normal.

"I was thinking about you today," her father said. Sarit heard him shuffling papers around in the background, so she knew he was still at work. "How was practice?"

Sarit took a deep breath. She was ready to pour out the whole awful truth. But her father was still talking.

"It just kills me not to be there with you girls," he said. "But I'm so happy when I think of you and Allie playing and practicing hard."

Sarit opened her mouth but didn't say anything.

"You are practicing hard, aren't you?" Dad asked.

"Of course," Sarit said quietly. That was her second lie of the day.

"I can't wait to see you girls play next month when I visit," Dad said. "You didn't forget, did you?"

Truthfully, Sarit had forgotten he was coming for a visit. But she didn't want to tell him that. She didn't want him to think she was forgetting him.

"I remember," she said. Now she was up to three lies. That had to be some kind of personal record.

Sarit heard a phone ringing in the background on her father's end. "I better answer that," her father said. "It could be important. I'll talk to you soon. Love you."

"I love you too, Dad," Sarit said. But her dad has already hung up. She set the phone back down beside her on the bed and flopped back against the pillows.

Now she felt even worse than before. She hadn't been able to tell her dad the truth, and on top of everything else she'd lied to him about practicing.

Sarit put her arm over her eyes. *It makes him so happy to think of Allie and me practicing*, she thought. *How can I tell him it makes me so sad?*

Chapter Four

TOO HARD TO PLAY

Sarit spent the next day at school dreading basketball practice. She could barely concentrate in any of her classes. When the last bell rang, Sarit walked with Allie down the crowded hallway toward the gym. They had practice after school every afternoon.

At the entrance to the locker room, Sarit stopped. She could hear the other Cowboys inside. Allie sighed impatiently. "Sarit, come on," she said. "We're already late."

Sarit hesitated. *Maybe I should go to practice*, she thought. *Dad wants me to. He said so yesterday on the phone.*

Just then, Coach Ritz walked out of his office. "There you are, Sarit. I need to talk to you," he said.

Sarit wasn't surprised the coach wanted to see her. She turned to Allie. "I'll catch up with you later," she told her sister.

"Okay," Allie said. She continued into the locker room to get ready for practice.

Sarit followed Coach Ritz back to his office and took a seat. He sat down on the edge of his desk and looked at her.

"You were really upset when you left practice yesterday, Sarit," the coach said sympathetically. "Do you want to talk about it?"

Sarit's eyes filled with tears. She swiped at them angrily. "I . . . I . . ." she stammered.

Coach Ritz handed her a tissue from the box on his desk. "I know it must be hard for you, not having your dad as the coach anymore," he said.

Sarit looked up in surprise. She hadn't expected her coach to understand what she was going through.

"But I bet your dad would want to see you out there on the court," Coach Ritz continued. He smiled encouragingly. "Let's go out there and have a practice that would make him proud."

Sarit shook her head. "I can't," she managed to say. She swallowed hard, trying not to cry. "I just don't want to play."

Coach Ritz looked at Sarit for a long time. Then he nodded. "Okay," he said. "That's your decision. Why don't you take some time, and think about what you really want to do."

Sarit nodded. Then she slowly stood up and walked out of the coach's office. Inside the gym, she could hear the rest of the basketball team warming up. Sarit paused, but shook her head and kept walking.

Once she was outside, Sarit headed for the athletic field. She knew she should be relieved that the coach had given her time off. But she just felt depressed.

She noticed a group of kids she didn't recognize playing a game of pick-up basketball at the end of the athletic field. Sarit wandered toward them and leaned against a light pole to watch.

A tall boy had the ball. He dribbled skillfully around the girl defending him, keeping the ball just out of her reach. He faked going right and then left. But he still couldn't shake his defender. The girl stayed with him, right up in his face. She held up her arms to block him. The boy crouched low and twisted left. The girl reached out to block him.

Pass, pass! Sarit thought. Then she shook her head. She was supposed to be done with basketball. But she couldn't take her eyes off the game.

As if he heard her, the boy glanced around the court. The defenders were crowding him. His back was to the basket, but he twisted hard, jumped, and shot. Sarit knew he could barely see the basket. The ball teetered on the rim and fell out.

The boy caught the rebound and passed to another girl on his team. She stretched her arms up high and leapt for the basket, going in for a lay-up. But a big defender on the other team stepped in front of her. The girl with the ball tripped and almost fell.

Foul! Sarit thought. She realized she was holding her breath. Her fists were clenched in excitement.

The girl caught herself and looked for the basket. A group of defenders stood in front of her, blocking her way. Her teammates were all being guarded.

In a split second, Sarit saw, the decision flashed through the girl's mind. She jumped for the basket and shot the ball right over the heads of her defenders. *Swish!* The ball soared from her hands straight through the basket.

"Yes!" Sarit cheered before she could stop herself. All the players turned to look at her.

Sarit felt her face turning red. "Uh, sorry," she mumbled, looking down at the ground. She turned and hurried away from the court. Her heart was pounding from the excitement of the game. As she wandered back toward home, Sarit realized that she was smiling for the first time in days.

Chapter Five

HARD TO WATCH

Sarit stopped outside the door of the gym. "Mom, I told you, I don't want to go," she said for the hundredth time that day.

Her mother put her hands on her hips. "Sarit, I've told you over and over. It's the first game of the season. We are going to watch," she said. She opened one of the big gym doors. "If you don't want to play on the team, the least you can do is support your sister."

Two weeks had passed since Sarit had run out of practice. Without basketball practice to keep her occupied, her days felt long and boring. Once, she'd turned on a basketball game after school, but had turned it right back off. She couldn't bring herself to watch, let alone play.

Her conversations with her father had only gotten more and more awkward. He kept asking her how practice was, and she kept lying. She'd never felt so terrible in her whole life.

Sarit followed her mother through the crowded gym. Mom found them a place to sit on an upper bleacher and they took their seats. Soon, the Cowboys ran onto the court. Everyone looked excited and ready to play. The opposing team, the Eagles, followed quickly behind.

Sarit saw Allie bouncing up and down on her toes and stretching as she waited for the game to start. Glancing up at the stands, Allie spotted them and waved excitedly. Mom waved back, but Sarit glared at her sister.

How can she be so heartless? Sarit thought angrily. *She acts like Dad is still standing on the sidelines coaching instead of Coach Ritz.*

Down on the court, the two opposing centers shook hands and faced off for the tip-off. The referee put her whistle to her lips. *Fweet!*

Both of the players leaped for the ball. The Cowboys' center tipped the ball to Allie, and the Cowboys took possession. Allie dribbled past a defender and headed for the basket.

Allie leaped into the air and took her shot. Air ball. The Cowboys' point guard was ready and jumped for the rebound right away. She shot and made the basket. Two points for the Cowboys.

Sarit thought about all the times her dad had made their team practice rebounding. *Looks like it paid off*, she thought.

The Eagles forward grabbed the ball and dribbled up the court. She passed to her team's center, who immediately passed it back. Sarit could see the Eagles forward looking around for someone to pass the ball to. But no one was open, and several of the Cowboys were bearing down on her.

The Eagles player jumped for the shot and missed. As she landed, she lost her balance and fell, but there was no foul.

Play continued. Allie had possession. She dribbled it up the court. Sarit couldn't help admiring her sister's fast, elegant moves. She easily evaded a defender. The audience cheered as Allie headed for the basket.

"Come on, Allie!" Mom shouted. She clapped her hands.

Allie shot the ball — a perfect *swoosh!* The players on the Cowboys bench cheered and high-fived. Sarit looked down at her own hands. No one remembered she was gone. No one missed her.

The Cowboys were leading 26-13 at halftime. When the buzzer sounded, Mom let out a happy sigh. "Well, this'll be an easy win," she said. "I'm going to get something to drink. You want anything, honey?"

Sarit shook her head. "No, thanks," she said. She watched as her mom made her way toward the snack counter. Down below, the Cowboys were all resting on the bench as Coach Ritz talked to the team.

Sarit felt a wave of loneliness wash over her. It was weird to be sitting in the bleachers by herself instead of on the bench with the rest of the team.

On the bench, all the players laughed at something Coach Ritz said. Allie was laughing too. *I can't believe her*, Sarit thought angrily. *She acts like she doesn't care about Dad at all. She just cares about playing.*

Sarit wanted to believe that, but she knew it wasn't true. They both cared.

So why am I the only one who feels so bad? she wondered.

Chapter Six

THE TRUTH COMES OUT

The Cowboys beat the Eagles in a great second half. Sarit had watched from the stands as the team celebrated. In the car on the way home, Allie chattered happily about the game. Mom seemed happy too.

"My daughter had the winning basket!" Mom exclaimed, smiling at Allie. "I'm so proud of you! The whole team played so well tonight. I can't believe Naomi scored on that three-point shot."

"I know!" Allie exclaimed. "And Anna's free throw in the fourth quarter was incredible. I thought I was going to have a heart attack."

"But then you stole it from the other center and came back up the court and scored with three seconds left on the buzzer!" Mom said. "32-29. Amazing."

Sarit sat silently in the backseat as her mom and sister recapped the game. Even though she was with her family, she'd never felt so lonely.

It's like they don't even know I'm here, she thought.

When they got home, Sarit went straight up to her room. She heard Mom and Allie talking downstairs, but she didn't want to hear what they were saying.

She took off her shoes and climbed into bed. She wanted to forget the whole day had happened.

Actually, I'd like to forget this whole year, Sarit thought. She wanted to wake up and have everything back the way it was before the divorce.

But when Sarit opened her eyes a few minutes later, she knew immediately that wasn't going to happen. Her mom was standing over her, holding the phone and looking furious.

Uh-oh, Sarit thought. She could tell she was in big trouble.

"Sarit, I called your father," Mom said. "This has gone on long enough. He didn't even know that you'd quit playing basketball."

Sarit felt sick to her stomach. She knew her dad was not going to be happy, especially about her lying to him. She reached out and took the phone. "Hi, Dad," she whispered.

"Hello, Sarit," her father said, sounding angry. "Your mother tells me you quit the basketball team two weeks ago. Have you been lying to me this whole time?"

Sarit swallowed the lump in her throat. "I guess," she mumbled.

"You guess?" Dad repeated. "I want an explanation, Sarit. Why would you quit the team and then lie about it?"

"Why should I tell you?" Sarit cried. "It's not like you're here to see me play or coach the —" Tears choked her, and she couldn't go on.

Her dad sighed. "I know I'm not there, Sarit," he said softly. "I wish I could be. But it's just not the way things worked out, sweetheart. When you run into a problem, you can't just quit. You need to work through it. That's what I taught you on the team."

"Then why couldn't you and Mom just work through your problems?" Sarit snapped. The words flew out of her mouth before she could stop them.

"That's not the same thing," Dad replied. He was starting to sound angry. "Your mother and I had serious problems that couldn't be worked out."

"Well, I don't get that," Sarit snapped at her father. "And you don't understand anything."

For a long moment, her father was silent. Then he said, "Sarit, honey, I don't want us to argue like this. I love you, and I wish I could be there. I think you should rejoin the basketball team. At least give the new coach a chance. I know it's not the same, but who knows? Maybe it will even be better some day."

"Yeah, maybe," Sarit replied.

"Promise me you'll at least think about it," Dad said.

"Okay," Sarit told him. But even as she said it, she didn't really mean it.

Chapter Seven

TOUGH LOVE

Sarit stared blankly at the basketball magazine in her hand. Then she sighed and tossed it onto her unmade bed. Her room was cluttered with books, magazines, and dirty clothes.

Sarit flopped down on her bed. Her mom was busy working, and Allie was at basketball practice. Sarit hadn't felt like leaving her room since she'd gotten off the phone with her father the day before.

Sarit thought about the last time she'd played basketball with her dad before he'd moved away. It had been right before he left for the airport.

Her dad had packed his bags and come out to the driveway to watch as she'd practiced shooting jump shots. She'd been crying, but hadn't wanted him to see that.

After a second, he'd snuck up behind her and stolen the ball, dribbling it down the driveway and back. He'd purposely fumbled it, giving her a chance to steal it, then dribbled between his legs and behind his back. Sarit had grabbed for it, laughing through her tears.

"Go in for a lay-up!" Dad had said. "Show me what you've got!" He'd tossed the ball into her hands and clapped as she dribbled up to the basket.

Now, alone in her room, Sarit flipped open her laptop and clicked on some old WNBA highlights. She stared dully at the figures on the screen, watching a talented player run past two guards and score an effortless three-pointer.

Just then, someone knocked at the door. Sarit opened it. Allie stood there, wearing her practice clothes and a determined expression.

"Can I come in?" Allie asked. Without waiting for an answer, she brushed past Sarit into the room.

"What are you doing here?" Sarit asked, closing the door behind her sister. "I thought you were supposed to be at basketball practice." She sat back down on the floor and picked up her laptop to watch some more WNBA clips.

Allie reached over her and closed the laptop, pulling it off her sister's lap. "Listen, Sarit, we have to talk," she said.

"Hey!" Sarit protested. She grabbed at her computer, but Allie held it away from her. "What's your problem? I was watching that."

Allie slid off the bed and scooted closer to Sarit on the floor. She looked her sister right in the eyes. "I am sick of you," she said.

Sarit blinked. "Gee, thanks a lot. Is that what you came here to tell me?" she said.

"Yes, it is," Allie replied. She stuck her chin out the way she did when she was really determined. "I'm sick and tired of you just moping around the house. You need to get your butt out on the court with the rest of us."

Sarit slumped down. "I already told you," she said. "I can't."

"No, you won't," Allie said. "There's a difference. Don't you think I miss Dad too? I miss him every single minute that I'm on the court."

"You don't act like it," Sarit snapped.

"Just because I'm not blaming Coach Ritz for something that isn't his fault doesn't mean I don't miss Dad," Allie replied. She slapped her hand down on the comforter. "Coach Ritz is a really good coach, and I love basketball," she said. "I may have lost Dad, but I'm not going to lose basketball too. And you shouldn't either."

Sarit just stared at her sister, her mouth hanging open. She'd never heard her sister talk like this before.

Allie wasn't finished. "Sarit, don't you get it? Basketball is what's helping me get over the divorce," she said. "When I'm out on the court, I can forget about Mom and Dad and just get into the game." Allie looked around Sarit's dark, messy room. "Besides, it's lonely in here," she said. "Don't you miss hanging out with the other girls?"

Sarit smiled a little. "Yeah," she admitted. "I miss them a ton. And I miss you, too." She took a deep breath. "It was really hard watching all of you guys playing without me yesterday. It was hard to watch from the stands."

Allie waited. Sarit looked at her sister and added, "And I've missed going to practice. I've missed basically everything. And Dad too."

"Me too," Allie said softly. She gave Sarit a hug. "And I'm really glad to hear you say you've missed everyone," she told Sarit. "Because I know they've missed you too."

Allie hopped up from the floor and walked over to open Sarit's bedroom door. The entire Cowboys basketball team was crowded together in the hallway.

Sarit's mouth fell open in surprise. She couldn't believe it. Everyone was smiling. She saw Anna and Hope wave at her tentatively.

"They all wanted to come over," Allie said. The girls nodded.

"The team hasn't been the same without you there," Anna said. "We told Allie we were going to come kidnap you and make you come back."

Anna stepped forward and thrust a basketball into Sarit's hands. "Get out here," she said with a grin. "I'm going to flatten you at three-on-three."

Chapter Eight

BACK ON THE COURT

Everyone was shouting and laughing as they pulled Sarit down the stairs and outside.

"You guys, slow down," Sarit kept saying. But she was happy to see her teammates. She knew her face was plastered with a silly grin.

Once they were out on the driveway, Naomi threw the ball to Sarit. Sarit had no choice but to catch it.

The minute the rough, warm leather hit her hands, Sarit felt herself relax. She just stood on the driveway, hugging the ball to her chest.

Allie jogged up the driveway to stand underneath the basketball hoop hanging over their garage door. "Me, Sarit, and Naomi against Anna, Hope, and Andrea!" she shouted. "Here, Sarit, pass it!" Allie waved her arms.

Sarit dribbled over. Andrea was guarding her, but Sarit spun around, looking for an open teammate. She passed the ball behind her back to Allie, who quickly took a shot and made it.

"Yes!" Sarit cheered happily. She couldn't believe how much she'd missed playing with her friends.

Anna caught the ball on the rebound and whirled around. Sarit was in front of her instantly, waving her arms to block Anna's shot.

Anna expression was intense and focused, and she was breathing hard, but she smiled. She boxed Sarit out and passed the ball to Hope.

Sarit's sneakers pounded the hard concrete as she raced across the driveway, almost colliding with Allie. She grabbed her twin to keep from falling, and both girls laughed, out of breath from the game. Allie flopped back on the grass.

The rest of the girls paused to catch their breath, too. Sarit saw her mom come out of her office. She looked over at the girls and gave Sarit a questioning look. She seemed to be waiting for something.

Sarit waved at her mom and gave her a thumbs-up. Mom smiled and waved back. She looked satisfied as she went back into her office.

Sarit bent over, hands on her knees, her heart pounding. She was a little out of shape after not practicing for two weeks. But she felt good. The dull, sad feeling was gone. Her mind was clear and alert. She knew it was because she was playing basketball again.

Allie jumped up from the grass. "Come on, you guys!" she yelled. "Let's finish this." She clapped her hands, and the girls took their positions on the court again.

Hope started with the ball. She tried to pass to Andrea, but Naomi was guarding her too tightly. Hope turned and passed it to Anna instead.

Andrea started dribbling up the side of the driveway. She almost lost the ball in some bushes, but she managed to hang on to it. Suddenly, Allie stuck out a hand and stole the ball. She shot but missed.

Anna caught the ball on the rebound. Guarding Anna was always hard, since she was so tall, but Sarit felt confident. Anna faked right, then left, but Sarit stuck with her. Anna tried to pass, but Sarit snatched the ball away.

"Whoohoo!" Allie yelled as Sarit dribbled up the driveway. The basketball hoop was right in front of her. For a second, Sarit imagined her dad standing on the sidelines. She could see him holding his clipboard and cheering.

She could practically hear him yelling, *Shoot!*

Allie was right, Sarit realized. Her dad wasn't there. But that didn't mean she couldn't play. Basketball was a part of her life, just like her dad was. No matter what. She didn't have to leave either of them behind.

Sarit jumped for the basket and shot. Everything felt right again. The moment her feet left the ground, she knew she'd made it.

AUTHOR BIO

Emma Carlson Berne has written more than a dozen books for children and young adults, including teen romance novels, biographies, and history books. She lives in Cincinnati, Ohio, with her husband, Aaron, her son, Henry, and her dog, Holly.

ILLUSTRATOR BIO

Katie Wood fell in love with drawing when she was very small. Since graduating from Loughborough University School of Art and Design in 2004, she has been living her dream working as a freelance illustrator. From her studio in Leicester, England, she creates bright and lively illustrations for books and magazines all over the world.

GLOSSARY

awkward (AWK-wurd) — difficult or embarrassing

dribble (DRIB-uhl) — to bounce a ball while running and keeping it under control

drills (DRILZ) — things done over and over again in order to learn a new skill

instructions (in-STRUHK-shuhnz) — directions on how to do something

rebound (RI-bound) — in basketball, to gain control of the ball after it has missed going in the basket

retrieve (ri-TREEV) — to get or bring something back

reverse (ri-VURSS) — to turn something around, upside down, or inside out

scrimmage (SKRIM-ij) — a game played for practice

DISCUSSION QUESTIONS

1. Why do you think it was hard for Sarit to watch her sister and teammates play, even though she quit the team? Talk about it.

2. Do you think seeing the kids playing basketball in the park helped Sarit? Why or why not?

3. How did Allie and the rest of the Cowboys help Sarit get back in the game? Talk about some other things they could have done.

WRITING PROMPTS

1. When Sarit's parents divorced, her dad moved across the country. Write about how you would react if something difficult like this happened to you.

2. Sarit has a special relationship with her father. What makes it so special? Write about your relationship with a parent.

3. Do you think Sarit made the right choice when she quit the basketball team? Why or why not?

BASKETBALL STARS

Women have been tearing up the basketball court since 1892 and continue to do so in the WNBA. Need more inspiration? Check out some of the most famous female basketball players of all time.

Babe Didrikson — One of the best female athletes of all time, Didrikson led her team to the Amateur Athletic Union basketball championships and is listed in the Guinness Book of Records as the most versatile female competitor thanks to her success in basketball, track and field, and golf.

Nera White — Known as the female Michael Jordan thanks to her fantastic maneuvering skills and athleticism, White was the first female basketball player to be inducted into the National Basketball Association Hall of Fame.

Lisa Leslie — Thanks to her status as a three-time MVP and two-time WNBA Champion, Leslie is one of the most popular female basketball stars in recent years. She is perhaps best known as the first player to have dunked in women's basketball.

Anne Donovan — Already a two-time gold medalist at the in the 1984 and 1988 Olympic Games, Donovan coached the U.S. women's basketball team to another gold medal in the 2008 Beijing Olympics. She is also the only player in history to have won the WNBA title both as a player and a coach.

Cheryl Miller — As a forward for the USC Trojans, Miller won two MVP awards and scored more than 3,000 career points, fifth all-time in NCAA history. She also earned a place in both the Basketball Hall of Fame and the Women's Basketball Hall of Fame.